Ultimate Collector's Guide

by Amy Ackelsberg

SCHOLASTIC INC.

ISBN 978-0-545-47770-3

12 11 10 9 8 7 6 5 4 3 2 1 12 13 14 15 16 17/0

Cover designed by Angela Jun and Carla Alpert
Interior designed by Angela Jun and Two Red Shoes Design
Printed in the U.S.A. 40
First printing, December 2012

MGA ENTERTAINMENT®

Table of Contents

Welcome to
Kat Lion's Roar
Marina Anchors
Sunny Side Up
Berry Jars 'N' Jam
Ember Flicker Flame
Spot Splatter Splash
Ace Fender Bender
Rosy Bumps 'N' Bruises
Dot Starlight
Mango Tiki Wiki
Misty Mysterious
Peanut Big Top
Harmony B. Sharp
Patch Treasurechest
Sahara Mirage
Prairie Dusty Trails
Coral Sea Shells

Dyna Might
Forest Evergreen
Swirly Figure Eight
Ivory Ice Crystals
Lalaloopsy
Land
Mittens Fluff 'N' Stuff
Holly Sleighbells
Suzette La Sweet
Blossom Flowerpot
Bea Spells-a-Lot
Jewel Sparkles
Tippy Tumblelina
Pillow Featherbed
Pickles B. L. T.
Crumbs Sugar Cookie
Lady Still Waiting
Toffee Cocoa Cuddles
Pepper Pots 'N' Pans
Bun Bun Sticky Icing
Cherry Crisp Crust
Sir Battle Scarred
Pix E. Flutters
Scoops Waffle Cone
Jelly Wiggle Jiggle
Bubble Smack 'N' Pop
Prince Handsome
Cinder Slippers
Twist E. Twirls
Toasty Sweet Fluff
Sugar Fruit Drops
Wacky Hatter
Snowy Fairest
Alice in Lalaloopsy Land
Pete R. Canfly
Scarlet Riding Hood

Meet the Lalaloopsy

Welcome to the whimsical world of Lalaloopsy! The Lalaloopsy were once rag dolls that magically came to life when their very last stitch was sewn. The dolls each have a special personality that comes from the fabrics that were used to make him or her.

In Lalaloopsy Land, the fun never ends! From tea parties and sleepovers to treasure hunts and silly adventures, the Lalaloopsy love to spend time with their friends. Each character is different, and each one has something special to share!

Join the Lalaloopsy on a journey through their fantastic world of imagination and silly surprises. This book is perfect to help you keep track of which Lalaloopsy you have—and which Lalaloopsy you need for your collection.

Bea Spells-a-Lot™

When Bea Spells-a-Lot's last stitch was sewn, she came to life knowing all the answers—or at least she thinks she does! She's a teacher's pet who always follows the rules. She loves to learn and is very talkative—which is great since she likes to share her knowledge with friends.

Sewn from:
A schoolgirl's uniform

Birthday: October 16 (Dictionary Day)

Pet: Owl

Likes: Big words

Dislikes: Wrong answers

Most likely to say:
"Repeat after me!"

Sewn from:
A baking apron

Birthday:
December 4 (National Cookie Day)

Pet: Mouse

Likes: Baking contests

Dislikes: Anything sour

Most likely to say:
"Pretty please with sprinkles on top?"

Crumbs Sugar Cookie is a super-sweet girl who loves to bake! She spends tons of time in her kitchen cooking up new creations, like cherry-chocolate cupcakes and strawberry sugar cookies. She loves having tea parties so she can invite her friends over for tasty treats.

Sewn from: An astronaut's space suit

Birthday: July 20 (First Man on the Moon)

Pet: Bird

Likes: Shooting stars

Dislikes: Cloudy skies

Most likely to say: "Let's shoot for the moon!"

Dot Starlight has a twinkling personality that shines even brighter than the sun, moon, and stars. She dreams of some day hopping on a rocket ship and soaring through space. But for now, she stays on the ground in Lalaloopsy Land with all her friends.

Jewel Sparkles™

Jewel Sparkles has a flair for the dramatic and nothing is ever too glittery for her. She's graceful and loves to dance, but she can also be a little bossy, especially when she's trying to plan the perfect party!

Sewn from: A princess's dress

Birthday: March 13 (Jewel Day)

Pet: Persian cat

Likes: Playing dress-up

Dislikes: Being ignored

Most likely to say: "Follow my lead!"

For Mittens Fluff 'n' Stuff there's nothing better than a snow day filled with sledding, ice skating, and a great big snowball fight with her friends. Afterward, she loves to snuggle up with her pet polar bear and drink hot cocoa by a cozy fire.

Sewn from: An Eskimo's scarf

Birthday: December 21 (First Day of Winter)

Pet: Polar bear

Likes: Warm clothes

Dislikes: Melting icicles

Most likely to say: "Want to go sledding?"

Peanut Big Top™

Sewn from:
A clown costume

Birthday: April 1
(April Fools' Day)

Pet: Elephant

Likes: Loud laughs

Dislikes: Using her "inside voice"

Most likely to say:
"Ta-da!"

Peanut Big Top has a special talent for making people laugh. She's never afraid to show her silly side, and she always has a trick up her sleeve. From dressing in crazy costumes to standing on her head, she'll do anything to turn a frown upside down!

Pillow Featherbed™

Sewn from:
A baby's blankie

Birthday: January 3
(Festival of Sleep Day)

Pet: Sheep

Likes: Milk and cookies

Dislikes: Alarm clocks

Most likely to say:
"Zzzzz."

Pillow Featherbed thinks that anytime is the right time for a nap. That's why she's always wearing her jammies! She's a bit of a night owl and she can be found up late reading a book or looking at the stars with Dot. She also throws great sleepover parties and loves a good pillow fight, just as long as she can get some rest after.

Spot Splatter Splash™

Spot Splatter Splash is a talented artist who loves bright colors and big ideas. She has a wild imagination and can find a creative way to make a big mess. One thing's for sure, it never gets boring when Spot is around!

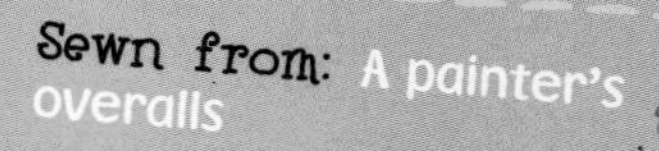

Sewn from: A painter's overalls

Birthday: October 25 (International Artist Day, also Picasso's Birthday)

Pet: Zebra

Likes: Eating spaghetti

Dislikes: Cleaning up

Most likely to say: "Here's my greatest masterpiece!"

Blossom Flowerpot™

Blossom Flowerpot has a special gift for making things grow. She can be found cheerfully digging in her garden and tending to her flowers. Her secret to growing prize-winning plants is sun, water, patience, and a whole lot of love!

Sewn from: A pair of gardener's gloves

Birthday: April 22 (Earth Day)

Pet: Butterfly

Likes: Worms

Dislikes: Cold weather

Most likely to say: "Have you hugged a tree today?"

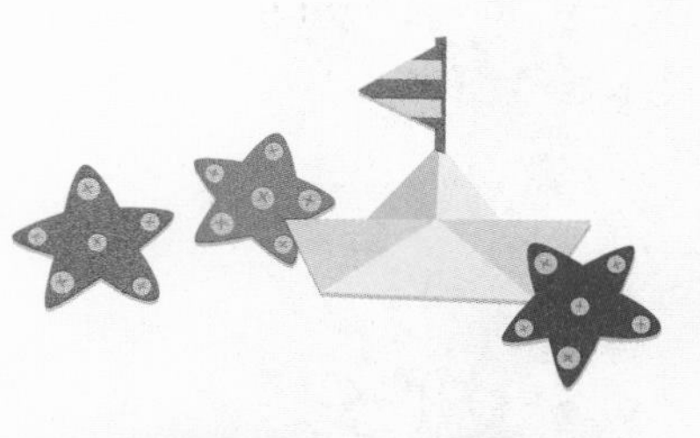

Sewn from: A sailor's uniform

Birthday: June 8 (World Ocean Day)

Pet: Whale

Likes: Lighthouses

Dislikes: Untying knots

Most likely to say: "Anchors away!"

Marina Anchors lives in a lighthouse on the coast of Lalaloopsy Land, and she always keeps her home shipshape. In fact, she loves organizing so much that she sometimes goes a bit overboard. Even though Marina loves the water, she doesn't know how to swim. That's why she's always wearing floaties or a lifesaver.

Pepper Pots 'n' Pans™

Pepper Pots 'n' Pans is the best chef in all of Lalaloopsy Land. No matter what is in Pepper's refrigerator, she can still create a gourmet meal. Her specialties are cheese soup and carrot sandwiches, but she also makes a great potato pie!

Tippy Tumblelina™

Tippy Tumblelina's toes are always tapping—it's hard to keep still when you're a ballet star. Sometimes she spins so fast that she tumbles to the ground. But Tippy's clumsiness never stops her from getting up and dancing some more!

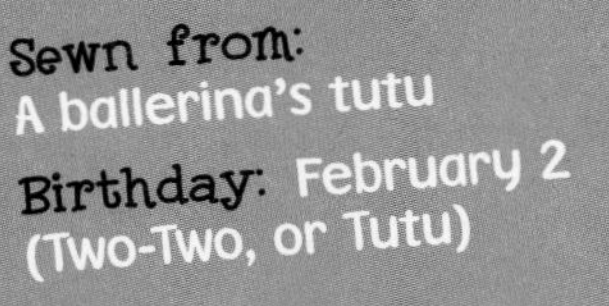

Sewn from:
A ballerina's tutu

Birthday: February 2
(Two-Two, or Tutu)

Pet: Swan

Likes: The spotlight

Dislikes: Getting dizzy

Most likely to say:
"This is tu-tu exciting!"

Sunny Side Up rises at dawn every morning to take care of the animals on her farm. She milks the cows, gathers eggs, and rakes hay. All that hard work is usually followed by a big blueberry pancake breakfast with her twin sister, Berry Jars 'n' Jam.

Berry Jars 'n' Jam™

Sewn from: A farmer's shirt and overalls

Birthday: October 12 (Old Farmers Day)

Pet: Cow

Likes: Cold milk

Dislikes: Rotten apples

Most likely to say: "Pancakes, anyone?"

Berry Jars 'n' Jam loves animals just as much as her twin sister, Sunny Side Up. She's sweet and kind, and always ready to lend a hand on the farm. And after a morning full of hard work, a blueberry pancake breakfast is just what she needs.

When Patch Treasurechest takes a trip, he needs an extra suitcase for the treasures he collects along the way! He digs for shiny gemstones in the mountains and finds smooth shells at the beach. He's always ready for an adventure . . . but he's not always good at reading maps.

Sahara Mirage™

Just like her name says, you never know where Sahara Mirage will pop up next. Sahara is afraid of the dark, but she's got a sparkling personality that can charm just about anyone.

Sewn from: A genie's veil

Birthday: January 13 (Make Your Dream Come True Day)

Pet: Camel

Likes: Making wishes come true

Dislikes: The dark

Most likely to say: "Dreamy!"

When her last stitch was sewn, Misty Mysterious came to life, only to disappear again. Luckily, it was just an illusion! She's a great friend who loves planning fun surprises. Sometimes she can get herself into tricky situations, but she always finds a way out.

Sewn from: A magician's cape

Birthday: March 24 (Houdini's Birthday)

Pet: Rabbit

Likes: Playing hide and seek

Dislikes: Sharing secrets

Most likely to say: "Abracadabra!"

Ace Fender Bender™

Ace Fender Bender is curious about how things work. He likes to tinker with everything from cars to bikes and boats, although he's not very good at putting them back together.

When Peppy Pom Poms's last stitch was sewn, she cartwheeled to life! She's an energetic performer who loves to look on the bright side. She's also got great team spirit and always roots for her friends . . . really, really loudly!

Coral Sea Shells™

Coral Sea Shells's favorite things are diving with dolphins and counting colorful fish. In fact, she loves the water so much she never wants to come up for air! Her greatest wish is to be a real mermaid and live a magical life under the sea!

Sewn from: A swimmer's bathing suit

Birthday: March 22 (World Water Day)

Pet: Blowfish

Likes: Seaweed salad

Dislikes: Being on land

Most likely to say: "Let's go for a dip!"

Sir Battlescarred™

Sir Battlescarred sprang to life ready for battle. He's a doer of good deeds, a righter of wrongs, and a fearless hero who'll stop at nothing to rescue a friend in trouble. One of these days, he will capture a castle!

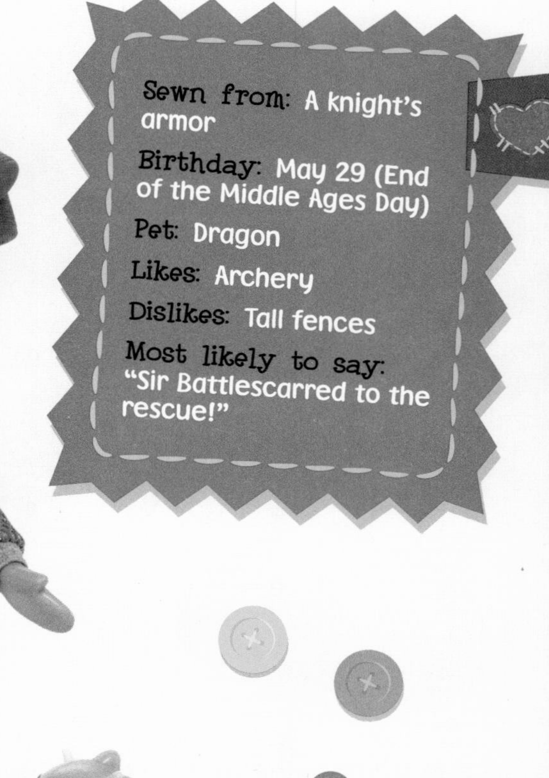

Lady Stillwaiting™

Lady Stillwaiting is simply lovely and sew polite. She's also a hopeless romantic who adores reading and writing poetry. She can often be seen waving from her balcony—even if no one is there to wave back!

Scarlet Riding Hood™

Sewn from:
Red Riding Hood's cape

Birthday: May 18
(Visit Your Relatives Day)

Pet: Wolf

Likes: Picking wildflowers

Dislikes: Getting lost

Most likely to say:
"My, what big teeth you have!"

Scarlet Riding Hood loves wearing red, wandering through the woods, and having picnics in the shade. She's a real sweetie who likes helping when her friends are in need.

When her last stitch was sewn, Snowy Fairest became the prettiest girl in all of Lalaloopsy Land! She's friendly and kind—a true beauty, inside and out. Her favorite things are juicy red apples and keeping the house spic and span!

Sewn from: Snow White's dress

Birthday: December 1 (Eat a Red Apple Day)

Pet: Squirrel

Likes: Juicy red apples

Dislikes: Messiness

Most likely to say: "Let's tidy up!"

When her last stitch was sewn, Pix E. Flutters flickered to life! She's an airy girl who wishes she could fly. She's easy to find when she plays hide-and-seek because she leaves a trail of glitter wherever she goes!

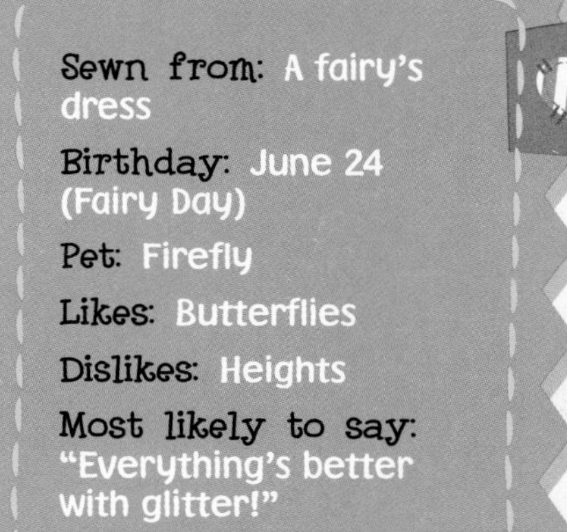

Sewn from: Cinderella's dress

Birthday: September 5 (Be Late For Something Day)

Pet: Mouse

Likes: Living happily ever after

Dislikes: Midnight

Most likely to say: "This is a dream come true!"

Cinder Slippers always has a lot of work to do, but she never misses a royal ball! She's kind and cheerful, even when things get tough. She likes wearing glass slippers . . . but only when they fit just right!

Swirly Figure Eight™

Sewn from:
An ice skater's costume

Birthday: January 20
(World Penguin Day)

Pet: Penguin

Likes: Ice

Dislikes: Falling down

Most likely to say:
"Watch me spin!"

Swirly Figure Eight is an ice-skating sensation. She's a true champion, but she didn't become one overnight. She thinks practice makes perfect—even if it does make her dizzy.

Holly Sleighbells™

Holly Sleighbells is a handy helper who loves to wrap presents—or anything else she can get her hands on. Her favorite thing to do is make a list and check it twice. If she could have one wish, she'd make every day a holiday!

Sewn from: An elf's costume

Birthday: December 3 (National Mistletoe Day)

Pet: Reindeer

Likes: Mistletoe

Dislikes: Empty stockings

Most likely to say: "Happy holidays!"

Ivory Ice Crystals™

Ivory Ice Crystals lives in an exquisite palace made entirely of ice. It has tall turrets frosted with icicles and gardens full of glowing ice sculptures. Once she invited her friends over for a fancy party with lots of dancing. She called it the Snow Ball!

Sewn from: A snow princess's dress

Birthday: February 27 (Polar Bear Day)

Pet: Polar bear

Likes: Lace

Dislikes: Thin ice

Most likely to say: "Do you like my icicle earrings?"

Suzette La Sweet™

Sewn from: A duchess's dress

Birthday: December 9 (National Pastry Day)

Pet: Poodle

Likes: Dressing up

Dislikes: Getting dirty

Most likely to say: "I need to put my feet up."

Suzette La Sweet has a special talent for relaxing, reclining, and lounging about. She's perfected the art of eating sweets and taking long walks in her garden. But it's not long before she's lounging on the couch again.

Rosy Bumps 'n' Bruises™

Sewn from:
A nurse's uniform

Birthday: May 12
(International Nurses Day)

Pet: Bear

Likes: Orange juice

Dislikes: Empty first aid kits

Most likely to say:
"I've got a bandage for that!"

Rosy Bumps 'n' Bruises has a solution for any problem, and it usually involves lots and lots of bandages! She fixes boo-boos with tender loving care, and always puts safety first.

Ember Flicker Flame™

Ember Flicker Flame to the rescue! Whether there's a real fire or a pet stuck in a tree, she's ready for the challenge! Sometimes Ember can get a little hotheaded, but it's only because she's sew passionate about things that are important to her—like her friends!

Sewn from: A firefighter's uniform

Birthday: May 4 (International Firefighters' Day)

Pet: Dalmatian

Likes: Spicy food

Dislikes: Unattended campfires

Most likely to say: "I'm fired up!"

Prairie Dusty Trails™

When her last stitch was sewn, Prairie Dusty Trails came to life ready to giddyup and go! When she's not riding off into the sunset, she's square dancing and doing rope tricks with her friends. Sometimes she can get a little rowdy, but her friends know how to reel her back in!

Sewn from: A cowgirl's vest

Birthday: August 13 (Annie Oakley's Birthday)

Pet: Cactus

Likes: Square dancing

Dislikes: Losing the trail

Most likely to say: "Yee-haw!"

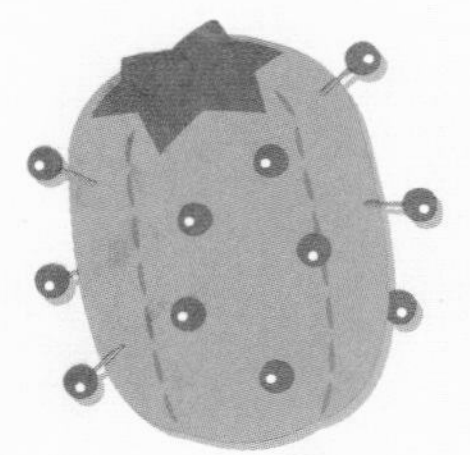

Sewn from:
A lumberjack's overalls

Birthday: September 26
(Lumberjack Day)

Pet: Beaver

Likes: Maple syrup

Dislikes: Forest fires

Most likely to say:
"Timmmberrr!"

Forest Evergreen is an expert tree climber, although once he's up, he usually can't figure out how to get down! He loves hiking in the woods and camping out under the stars. He also likes to cook with his secret ingredient: maple syrup!

Toffee Cocoa Cuddles™

Sewn from: A chocolate box

Birthday: June 11 (National Hug Day)

Pet: Chocolate Lab

Likes: Chocolates

Dislikes: Lots of attention

Most likely to say: "How sweet!"

Toffee Cocoa Cuddles is sew kind and incredibly cute. She loves to show her friends how much she cares by giving them lots and lots of hugs. She also likes to send her friends a nice note, along with some candy and roses.

Charlotte Charades never says a word, but she sure likes to make funny faces and act out silly skits to entertain her friends. She'll go a long way to make them laugh, like the time she pretended to slip on a banana peel while she was walking her invisible pet!

Mango Tiki Wiki™

Mango Tiki Wiki is a carefree beach girl who loves to feel the sand beneath her feet. When she's not making sand castles or carving coconuts, she's listening to music and dancing under palm trees. She also likes fresh flowers and fruit.

Sewn from: A dancer's grass skirt

Birthday: May 2 (Play Your Ukulele Day)

Pet: Pineapple bird

Likes: Hula dancing

Dislikes: Rainy days

Most likely to say: "Aloha!"

Pickles B.L.T.™

Sewn from:
A waitress's uniform

Birthday: May 21
(National Waiter and Waitress Day)

Pet: Hot dog

Likes: Pickle burgers

Dislikes: Having too much on her plate

Most likely to say:
"What'll it be, sugar?"

Pickles B.L.T. is a multi-talented multitasker who can get any job done in no time. She's usually in a hurry, but she always has time to take good care of her friends. If they're having a bad day, she serves them an extra pickle burger with a big smile!

Sewn from:
A pair of moccasins

Birthday: April 27
(Tell a Story Day)

Pet: Bears

Likes: Animals

Dislikes: The city

Most likely to say:
"Once upon a time . . ."

When Feather Tell-a-Tale's last stitch was sewn, she came to life telling stories. From legends and myths to silly tales and jokes, she keeps her friends on the edge of their seats and hanging on every word.

Harmony B. Sharp™

Harmony B. Sharp has a showstopping personality and loves to act, dance, and sing. She's forever belting out a tune or starring in a one-person show, even if she misses a note or two. And she loves having her pet kitty join in, too!

Sewn from: A singer's dress

Birthday: March 27 (International Theater Day)

Pet: Kitty

Likes: High notes

Dislikes: Sharing the spotlight

Most likely to say: "The show must go on!"

Dyna Might is a fearless superhero. There's no mission too big for her to tackle—especially if she's got on her pink-powered goggles and her sidekick raccoon!

Kat Jungle Roar™

Sewn from:
A safari outfit

Birthday: September 4
(National Wildlife Day)

Pet: Lion

Likes: Exploring

Dislikes: Being bored

Most likely to say:
"The elephant is known for its long trunk."

Kat Jungle Roar was sewn from a safari outfit. She's an adventure seeker who loves discovering new places. She loves using binoculars and hiding in bushes so she can sneak up on animals and observe them in their natural habitats.

Meet the Lalaloopsy Littles

The Lalaloopsy Littles are the adorable younger siblings of the Lalaloopsy dolls. They may be little, but they each have a big personality!

These terrific tots are always up for adventure and love to tag along with their older siblings wherever they go. Curiosity seems to always get the Littles in trouble, so it's a good idea to keep a close eye on them.

Bundles Snuggle Stuff™

Bundles Snuggle Stuff is sew playful and cuddly cute. She's always ready for winter fun with her big sister, Mittens. She especially loves to throw snowballs when she's not supposed to!

Sewn from: An Eskimo's scarf
Birthday: January 6 (Cuddle Up Day)
Pet: Bear
Likes: Eating ice cream
Dislikes: Staying indoors
Most likely to say: *"Wheee!"*

Sprinkle Spice Cookie™

Sprinkle Spice Cookie will do anything for a treat! She usually sticks close to her big sister, Crumbs, especially when a fresh batch of cookies is about to come out of the oven.

Sewn from: A baker's clothes
Birthday: May 15 (National Chocolate Chip Day)
Pet: Mouse
Likes: Licking batter from the bowl
Dislikes: Burned cookies
Most likely to say: "Yum! Yum!"

Specs Reads-a-Lot™

Specs Reads-a-Lot is a little genius who loves math and spelling big words with her alphabet blocks. She loves getting gold stars and eating apples.

Sewn from: A schoolgirl's uniform
Birthday: March 14
(Pi Day, also Einstein's Birthday)
Pet: Worm
Likes: Gold stars
Dislikes: Broken crayons
Most likely to say: "One, two, three!"

Squirt Lil' Top™

Squirt Lil' Top sprang to life doing circus tricks! She's a show-off and a bit of a daredevil, just like her big sister, Peanut. Her favorite moves are cartwheels and somersaults!

Sewn from: A clown's costume
Birthday: January 19 (National Popcorn Day)
Pet: Peanut
Likes: Carnivals
Dislikes: Gravity
Most likely to say: "Boing! Boing!"

Trinket Sparkles™

Trinket Sparkles likes being the center of attention. When she goes out to play, she can usually be found wearing frilly dresses, glittery jewels, and towering tiaras—all at the same time!

Sewn from: A princess's dress
Birthday: May 24 (Wear a Tiara Day)
Pet: Kitten
Likes: Ruffles
Dislikes: The color gray
Most likely to say: "*Ooo, pretty!*"

Scribbles Splash™

Scribbles Splash's personality is as bright and colorful as the finger paint she uses. Just like her sister, Spot, Scribbles is creative and fun, and loves to try new things. Once, she even tried to paint with her feet!

Sewn from: A painter's overalls
Birthday: January 28 (Jackson Pollock's Birthday)
Pet: Giraffe
Likes: Rainbows
Dislikes: Coloring inside the lines
Most likely to say: "Whoopsie!"

Matey Anchors™

Matey Anchors came to life ready to set sail. He's captain of a fleet of paper sailboats and would never abandon a ship, unless it's time for dinner with his sister, Marina.

Sewn from: A sailor's uniform
Birthday: July 1 (National Boating Day)
Pet: Crab
Likes: Bathtime
Dislikes: Rough seas
Most likely to say: "Ahoy!"

Pita Mirage™

Pita Mirage and her sister, Sahara, have the gift for charming everyone they meet. Pita loves granting wishes, but she often gets mixed up. Once, her friend Bundles wished for HUGS, but Pita gave her BUGS instead!

Sewn from: A genie's veil
Birthday: August 11 (Play in the Sand Day)
Pet: Snake
Likes: Playing the flute
Dislikes: Being without her magic carpet
Most likely to say: "Wishes, anyone?"

Blanket Featherbed™

Blanket Featherbed loves to stay up late and will do anything to avoid going to bed. One time she tried to hide in her closet until morning, but her sister, Pillow, found her! When she does finally go to sleep, she snores . . . really loudly!

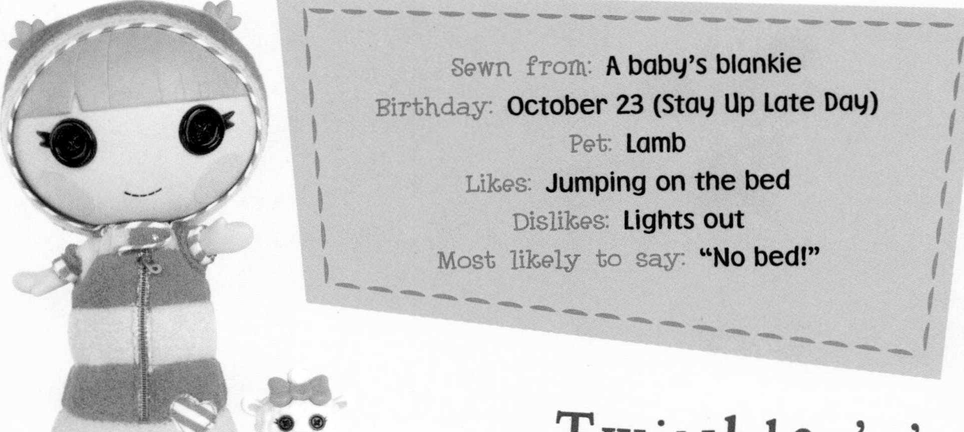

Sewn from: A baby's blankie
Birthday: October 23 (Stay Up Late Day)
Pet: Lamb
Likes: Jumping on the bed
Dislikes: Lights out
Most likely to say: "No bed!"

Twinkle 'n' Flutters™

Twinkle 'n' Flutters is feisty and fearless. She loves to make mischief, but it's easy to tell when she's up to something—she always gets a twinkle in her eye!

Sewn from: A fairy's dress
Birthday: February 2 (Sneeze Day)
Pet: Firefly
Likes: Fireworks
Dislikes: Bumpy landings
Most likely to say: *"Achoo!"*

Stumbles Bumps 'n' Bruises™

Stumbles Bumps 'n' Bruises is always worried that she's coming down with something! She's the perfect patient for her sister, Rosy, because she loves wearing bandages.

Sewn from: A nurse's uniform
Birthday: February 7 (Love Your Patients Day)
Pet: Bear
Likes: X-rays
Dislikes: Shots
Most likely to say: "Ouchie!"

Whiskers Lion's Roar™

Whiskers Lion's Roar might have a ferocious-sounding growl, but she's a real sweetie. She loves to sneak up on her friends. Then, she pounces and gives them a big hug!

Sewn from: A safari outfit
Birthday: October 29 (National Cat Day)
Pet: Lion cub
Likes: Napping in the sun
Dislikes: Taking a bath
Most likely to say: *"Grrr!"*

Trouble Dusty Trails™

Trouble Dusty Trails is a lil' buckaroo with a big attitude. She likes to be in charge and stomps her feet when she doesn't get her way. Her hobbies are flashing her sheriff's badge and taming the wild, wild West!

Sewn from: A cowgirl's vest
Birthday: May 1 (Law Day)
Pet: Horse
Likes: Rodeos
Dislikes: Bad guys
Most likely to say: "Giddyup!"

Tricky Mysterious™

Tricky Mysterious is an excellent magician's assistant. She loves making up magic words and waving her wand, but before you know it . . . she disappears!

Sewn from: A magician's cape
Birthday: February 29 (Leap Day)
Pet: Bunny
Likes: Being onstage
Dislikes: Stage fright
Most likely to say: "Presto!"

yum

Mini Lalaloopsy

These sew sweet mini dolls can fit in your pocket and are perfect to take on-the-go for a magical adventure! Whether they're playing hide-and-seek, taking a swim in a rainwater puddle, or resting in the shade of a flower, these little friends are in a world all their own.

The mini Lalaloopsy that are on the next few pages are extra sweet since they are only available in mini form—proving that good things really do come in small packages!

Bun Bun Sticky Icing™

Bun Bun Sticky Icing is a true delight. She has a rich personality and a delicious sense of humor. Sometimes she goes over-the-top with sweetness. Once, she made a cinnamon bun banana split with hot fudge and sprinkles!

Sewn from: A cinnamon roll
Birthday: October 4 (National Cinnamon Bun Day)
Pet: Snail
Likes: Frosting
Dislikes: Empty sugar bowls
Most likely to say: "Life is sweet!"

Cherry Crisp Crust™

Sewn from: A cherry pie
Birthday: February 20 (National Cherry Pie Day)
Pet: Blackbird
Likes: The color red
Dislikes: Sour treats
Most likely to say: "Life is just a bowl of cherries!"

Cherry Crisp Crust knows how to make her friends feel their best. She's warmhearted, comforting, and super-upbeat. She spends her days baking prize-winning pies, and she thinks everything tastes better with ice cream on top!

Sugar Fruit Drops™

Sugar Fruit Drops can be a bit of a handful. She loves juicy gossip and will dish about everything that goes on in Lalaloopsy Land. Once, she told Cherry about a party Scoops was planning, and it spoiled the surprise!

Sewn from: A gum drop
Birthday: February 15 (National Gum Drop Day)
Pet: Mouse
Likes: Spicy stories
Dislikes: Getting stuck
Most likely to say: "I love you to bits."

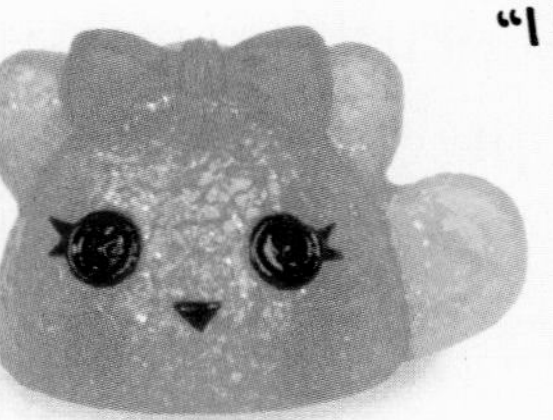

Scoops Waffle Cone™

Scoops Waffle Cone is fun and super-stylish. She loves to dress in layers and always has the scoop on the latest fashions. She's cool under pressure, but can sometimes seem a little chilly. To cheer her up, all it takes is one hug—she just melts!

Sewn from: A bowl of Neapolitan ice cream

Birthday: July 19 (National Ice Cream Day)

Pet: Cat

Likes: Accessorizing

Dislikes: Getting mixed up

Most likely to say: "What a treat!"

Jelly Wiggle Jiggle™

Sewn from:
A bowl of lime gelatin
Birthday: July 12 (Eat Something Jiggly Day)
Pet: Turtle
Likes: The jitterbug
Dislikes: Sitting still
Most likely to say:
"What lime is it?"

When her last stitch was sewn, Jelly Wiggle Jiggle danced to life! She's quite the character and loves silly stories. She tries to keep a straight face when she's telling jokes—but her friends see right through her! Then she laughs so hard that she jiggles.

Bubble Smack 'n' Pop™

Sewn from: A stick of bubble gum

Birthday: February 3 (Bubble Gum Day)

Pet: Bear

Likes: Pink

Dislikes: Sticky situations

Most likely to say: "That's adorabubbles!"

Bubble Smack 'n' Pop is a popular girl with a bubbly personality. She's usually bursting with good news or singing a snappy song. She likes to travel and is always popping in and out of town. But when she's hanging out with her friends, she definitely sticks around.

Toasty Sweet Fluff™

Sewn from:
A fresh marshmallow

Birthday: August 10 (National S'mores Day)

Pet: Bunny

Likes: Dandelions

Dislikes: Roughing it

Most likely to say:
"Can I have s'more hugs?"

Toasty Sweet Fluff will lighten your day with her soft touch. She's sew huggable, it's hard to resist giving her a squeeze! She's a great swimmer, and her favorite thing is to float on the water. Then she looks up at the sky and imagines what it would be like to live in the clouds.

Twist E. Twirls™

Twist E. Twirls is a jump rope fanatic and exercise expert. She's flexible and can coil herself into any position. She's also superstrong and likes to stretch herself to the limit. When it comes time to show off her moves, she whips up a new routine with dazzling twists and turns.

Sewn from: Red licorice

Birthday: April 12 (National Licorice Day)

Pet: Butterfly

Likes: Twists and turns

Dislikes: Straight lines

Most likely to say: "I need to unwind."

Curls 'n' Locks™

Sewn from: Goldilocks's dress
Birthday: October 29 (National Oatmeal Day)
Pet: Three pet bears
Likes: Porridge
Dislikes: Small beds
Most likely to say: "This is just right!"

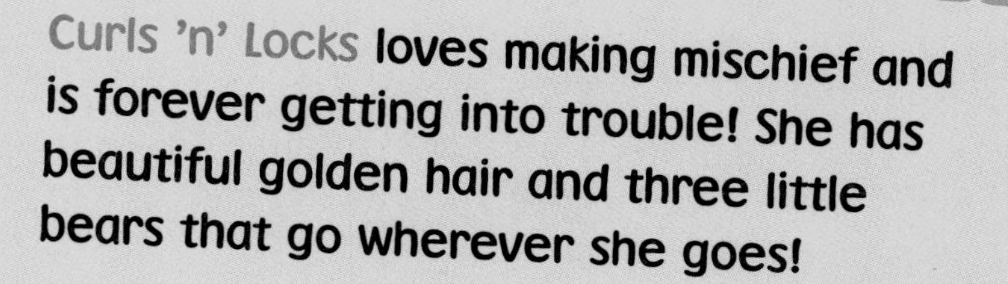

Curls 'n' Locks loves making mischief and is forever getting into trouble! She has beautiful golden hair and three little bears that go wherever she goes!

Little Bah Peep™

Sewn from: Little Bo Peep's bonnet

Birthday: February 20 (Love Your Pet Day)

Pet: Two sheep

Likes: Taking long walks

Dislikes: Losing things

Most likely to say: "Follow me!"

Little Bah Peep is sweet and gentle, and she loves animals. She can be a little careless with her sheep though. Once, she took a nap under a shady tree, and all the sheep wandered off. Luckily, they found their way home again.

Pete R. Canfly™

Pete R. Canfly loves to play games. He's mischievous and a bit of a show-off, but he's quick to help his friends if they're in trouble. He likes to pretend he can fly . . . although he often ends up crashing!

Sewn from: Peter Pan's hat
Birthday: August 12 (International Youth Day)
Pet: Crocodile
Likes: Adventure
Dislikes: Growing up
Most likely to say: "I'll never grow up!"

Tuffet Miss Muffet™

Sewn from: Little Miss Muffet's apron
Birthday: March 14 (Save a Spider Day)
Pet: Spider
Likes: Peace and quiet
Dislikes: Surprise parties
Most likely to say: "Yikes!"

Every morning, Tuffet Miss Muffet sits on a cozy cushion and eats a healthy snack. She keeps to herself and is easily startled. In fact, she's afraid of almost everything . . . everything except big spiders!

Alice in Lalaloopsyland™

Alice in Lalaloopsyland is either too tall or too small. Whichever one it is, it doesn't make any sense at all! When she's looking for adventure, she just needs to doze, and then down, down, down the rabbit hole she goes!

Sewn from: Alice in Wonderland's dress

Birthday: June 12 (Red Rose Day)

Pet: White rabbit

Likes: Talking flowers

Dislikes: Boring schoolbooks

Most likely to say: "How curious!"

Wacky Hatter™

Wacky Hatter is perfectly odd. He loves silly riddles and playing musical chairs. He also likes to spout poetry at tea time.

Sewn from:
The Mad Hatter's hat

Birthday: September 15 (Make a Hat Day)

Pet: Cat

Likes: Unbirthdays

Dislikes: Rude questions

Most likely to say:
"More tea?"

Prince Handsome™

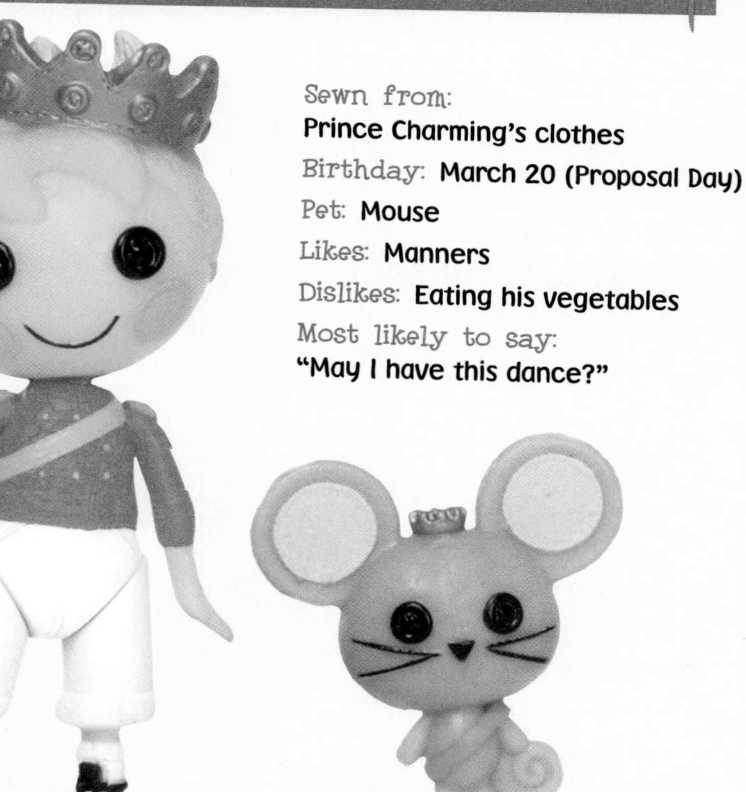

Sewn from:
Prince Charming's clothes

Birthday: March 20 (Proposal Day)

Pet: Mouse

Likes: Manners

Dislikes: Eating his vegetables

Most likely to say:
"May I have this dance?"

It's easy to tell when Prince Handsome's around—a trio of trumpets announce his arrival! He's a charming fellow with dashing good looks, although he doesn't always remember his manners. He once invited Cinder Slippers to a royal ball, but she turned him down because he forgot to say 'please'!

Cotton Hoppalong™

Cotton Hoppalong is a lively girl who's always leaping and bouncing. She always gets parties hopping and loves candy—though she may not want to share.

Sewn from: A pair of bunny slippers

Birthday: March 21 (First Day of Spring)

Pet: Chick

Likes: Bouncing

Dislikes: Sharing candy

Most likely to say: "Hippity hop!"

Sprouts Sunshine™

Sewn from: **A flower basket**

Birthday: **June 3 (National Egg Day)**

Pet: **Bunny**

Likes: **Jellybeans**

Dislikes: **Cloudy days**

Most likely to say: **"Let's hunt for eggs!"**

Sprouts Sunshine always has a spring in her step and likes to hide eggs wherever she goes. She can be a little shy, and when she meets someone new, it takes a while for her to come out of her shell. She loves flowers, fashionable hats, and having picnics with her friends!

Candy Broomsticks™

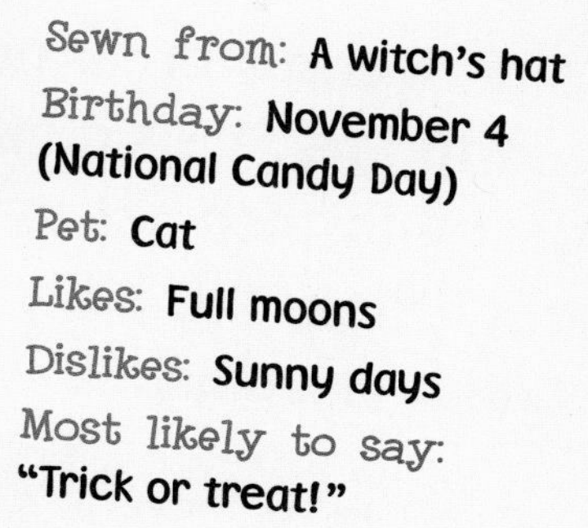

Sewn from: A witch's hat

Birthday: November 4 (National Candy Day)

Pet: Cat

Likes: Full moons

Dislikes: Sunny days

Most likely to say: "Trick or treat!"

When her last stitch was sewn, Candy Broomsticks came to life casting spells! She's a great host and loves to invite her friends to tour her haunted house. She tells them spooky stories and mixes special potions. Her favorite holiday is Halloween, but she wears a costume all year round!

Scraps Stitched 'N' Sewn™

One dark and stormy night, Scraps Stitched 'n' Sewn jolted to life. She's a monstrously shy girl with a frightful fashion sense. She can also be shockingly sweet. Once, she gave half of her Halloween treats to Candy Broomsticks when Candy lost all of hers.

Sewn from: **Scraps and a bolt of lightning**
Birthday: **August 30 (Mary Shelley's Birthday)**
Pet: **Dog**
Likes: **Thunderstorms**
Dislikes: **Frilly dresses**
Most likely to say: **"Rain, rain, come my way."**

Collect them all!

There are *sew* many different kinds of Lalaloopsy to collect—including Littles, minis, Silly Hair, soft dolls, and micros. With that many different dolls, it can be a challenge to keep tabs on your whole collection.

To help you keep track, you can use the check box next to each doll's name—place a check in the box if you already have the doll or a heart if you'd love to have it!

Lalaloopsy

☐ Bea Spells-a-Lot

☐ Crumbs Sugar Cookie

☐ Dot Starlight

☐ Jewel Sparkles

☐ Mittens Fluff 'n' Stuff

☐ Peanut Big Top

☐ Pillow Featherbed

☐ Spot Splatter Splash

☐ Blossom Flowerpot

☐ Marina Anchors

☐ Pepper Pots 'n' Pans

☐ Tippy Tumblelina

☐ Sunny Side Up

☐ Berry Jars 'n' Jam

☐ Patch Treasurechest

☐ Sahara Mirage

☐ Misty Mysterious

☐ Ace Fender Bender

☐ Peppy Pom Poms

☐ Coral Sea Shells

☐ Sir Battlescarred

Lalaloopsy

☐ Lady Stillwaiting

☐ Scarlet Riding Hood

☐ Snowy Fairest

☐ Pix E. Flutters

☐ Cinder Slippers

☐ Swirly Figure Eight

☐ Holly Sleighbells

☐ Ivory Ice Crystals

☐ Suzette La Sweet

☐ Rosy Bumps 'N' Bruises

☐ Ember Flicker Flame

☐ Prairie Dusty Trails

☐ Forest Evergreen

☐ Toffee Cocoa Cuddles

☐ Charlotte Charades

☐ Mango Tiki Wiki

☐ Pickles B. L. T.

☐ Feather Tell-a-Tale

☐ Harmony B. Sharp

☐ Dyna Might

☐ Kat Jungle Roar

Lalaloopsy Littles

☐ Bundles Snuggle Stuff

☐ Sprinkle Spice Cookie

☐ Specs Reads-a-Lot

☐ Squirt Lil' Top

☐ Trinket Sparkles

☐ Scribbles Splash

☐ Matey Anchors

☐ Pita Mirage ☐ Blanket Featherbed ☐ Twinkle N. Flutters

☐ Stumbles Bumps 'N' Bruises ☐ Whiskers Lion's Roar

☐ Trouble Dusty Trails ☐ Tricky Mysterious

Mini Lalaloopsy

Series 1

☐ Pillow Featherbed

☐ Crumbs Sugar Cookie

☐ Mittens Fluff 'n' Stuff

☐ Peanut Big Top

☐ Spot Splatter Splash

☐ Jewel Sparkles

☐ Dot Starlight

☐ Bea Spells-a-Lot

☐ Sunny Side Up

☐ Berry Jars 'n' Jam

☐ Blossom Flowerpot

☐ Tippy Tumblelina

☐ Pepper Pots 'n' Pans

☐ Misty Mysterious

☐ Sahara Mirage

☐ Marina Anchors

Mini Lalaloopsy

Series 3

☐ Mittens's Sleepover

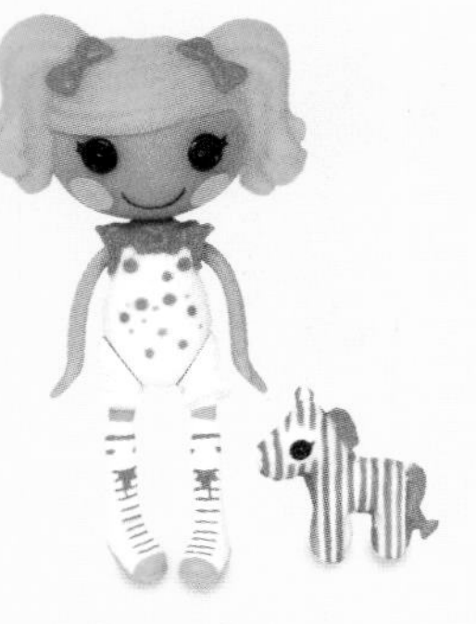

☐ Spot Paints Purple

☐ Peanut's New Tricks

☐ Pillow's Storytime

☐ Sir Battlescarred

☐ Lady Stillwaiting

☐ Ace Fender Bender

☐ Swirly Figure Eight

Series 4

☐ Bea Plays in the Rain

☐ Marina's Beach Day

☐ Pepper Cooks Up Fun

☐ Mittens Bundles Up

☐ Marina's Sea Adventure

☐ Misty's Full of Tricks

☐ Sahara's Desert Dream

☐ Pepper's Midnight Snack

Mini Lalaloopsy

Series 5

☐ Peanut's Elephant Act

☐ Crumbs's Tea Time

☐ Jewel's Bubble Bath

☐ Lady Writes a Poem

☐ Spot's New Masterpiece

☐ Patch's Treasure Hunt

☐ Forest Evergreen

☐ Ember Flicker Flame

☐ Peppy Pom Poms

☐ Berry's Blueberry Party

☐ Blossom's A Busy Bee

☐ Suzette La Sweet

☐ Rosy Bumps 'N' Bruises

☐ Prairie Dusty Trails

☐ Toffee Cocoa Cuddles

Mini Lalaloopsy Tales

Series 7

☐ Scarlet Riding Hood

☐ Little Bah Peep

☐ Tuffet Miss Muffe

☐ Curls 'n' Locks

☐ Pix E. Flutters

☐ Coral Sea Shells

☐ Pete R. Canfly

☐ Snowy Fairest

Mini Lalaloopsy Shoppes™

Series 8

☐ Cherry Crisp Crust

☐ Bun Bun Sticky Icing

☐ Scoops Waffle Cone

☐ Jelly Wiggle Jiggle

☐ Peanut Big Top Sew Sleepy

☐ Peppy Pom Poms Sew Sleepy

☐ Crumbs Sugar Cookie Sew Sleepy

☐ Pix E. Flutters Sew Sleepy

Mini Lalaloopsy Candy Cute™

Series 9

☐ Bubble Smack 'n' Pop

☐ Toasty Sweet Fluff

☐ Sugar Fruit Drops

☐ Twist E. Twirls

Mini Lalaloopsy Exclusives

☐ Cotton Hoppalong

☐ Sprouts Sunshine

☐ Holly Sleighbells

☐ Scraps Stitched 'n' Sewn

☐ Candy Broomsticks

☐ Ivory Ice Crystals

Silly Funhouse

☐ Ace Fender Bender

☐ Blossom Flowerpot and Charlotte Charades

☐ Jewel Sparkles

☐ Marina Anchors

☐ Peanut Big Top and Ember Flicker Flame

Lalaloopsy Silly Hair

☐ Bea Spells-a-Lot

☐ Crumbs Sugar Cookie

☐ Jewel Sparkles

☐ Mittens Fluff 'n' Stuff

☐ Peanut Big Top

☐ Pix E. Flutters

☐ Spot Splatter Splash

☐ Suzette La Sweet

Lalaloopsy Soft Dolls

☐ Bea Spells-a-Lot ☐ Crumbs Sugar Cookie

☐ Mittens Fluff 'n' Stuff ☐ Jewel Sparkles

☐ Patch Treasurechest

☐ Peanut Big Top

☐ Pillow Featherbed

☐ Spot Splatter Splash

Micros
Series 1
Series 2

Series 3
MILK
JaM
Series 4

Playsets

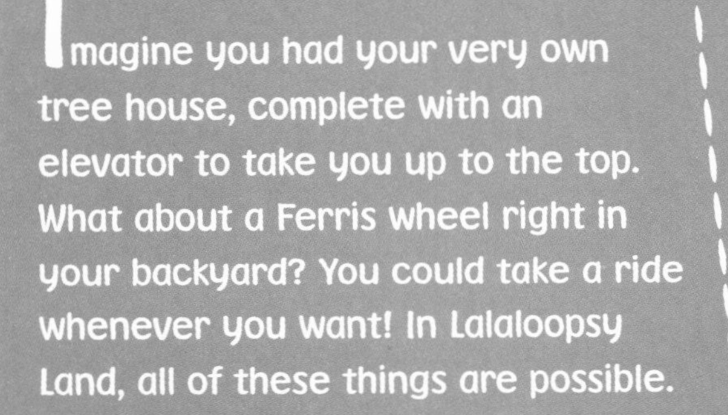

Imagine you had your very own tree house, complete with an elevator to take you up to the top. What about a Ferris wheel right in your backyard? You could take a ride whenever you want! In Lalaloopsy Land, all of these things are possible.

These adorable mini Lalaloopsy playsets and accessories mean even more ways to spend time with your favorite Lalaloopsy friends. The possibilities for fun are endless.

Crumbs's Tea Party

Crumbs Sugar Cookie loves inviting her friends over to sip tea and taste the yummy treats she bakes. This adorable Mini Lalaloopsy Crumbs's Tea Party playset is where she serves up the perfect party! When it's time for tea, the Lalaloopy get all dressed up. They eat tea cakes, share delightful conversation, and plan their next adventures in Lalaloopsy Land—yum! Thanks, Crumbs!

Pillow's Sleepover Party

When Pillow Featherbed dreams of the perfect night, she imagines a sleepover party! With Pillow's Sleepover Party playset, she's ready to host a fabulous sleepover for her friends! First, they'll set up their sleeping bags and change into their pajamas. Then, each girl shares a special surprise! Once, Peanut Big Top brought popcorn and a movie. Another time, Jewel Sparkles brought dress-up clothes. When it's time for bed, they're out like a light! Sweet dreams, everyone.

Peanut's Ferris Wheel

Step right up and take a ride on the Ferris wheel with Peanut Big Top and all her Lalaloopsy friends! Round and round they go—they're so high up that they can see all of Lalaloopsy Land. *Whee!* One ride is never enough.

Whether she's going to a party, a birthday bash, or for a walk in the park, Jewel Sparkles loves to get dressed up! With Jewel's Primpin' Party playset, she can try on new outfits, make sure her tiara is on just right, or simply make silly faces at herself in the mirror! She's got all the tools she needs to make herself look perfect, perfect, perfect!

Treehouse

The Mini Lalaloopsy Treehouse playset is a fantastically fun place to hang out and play pretend with all your friends! Patch Treasurechest loves to climb to the top and check out the views from the crow's nest. If he's lucky, he'll spot some treasure! Spot Splatter Splash likes to design exciting obstacle courses for her friends. First, they run to the trunk and spin around, and then they ride the elevator straight up to the clubhouse. Then it's down the zip line on the tire swing! It's a race to see who'll finish first!

When it's time for a break, the Lalaloopsy and their pets swing from the branches and relax in the hammocks. One time, Pillow Featherbed even hosted a sleepover right in the tree! She and her friends read bedtime stories, had milk and cookies, and fell asleep under the stars.

Berry's Kitchen

Follow the sweet smells to the Berry Jars 'n' Jam's Kitchen playset! Berry loves making huge stacks of pancakes with blueberry sauce. One time, Berry and her friend Pepper Pots 'n' Pans had a cook-off to see who could make the most delectable dishes. Berry made strawberry walnut salad, and Pepper made pepperoni pizza. Who won? It was a tie!

Bea's School Bus

Beep! Beep! This bus brakes for fun! Ride along with your Lalaloopsy friends on Bea Spells-a-Lot's school bus. Adventure awaits as she winds her way through Lalaloopsy Land, picking up pals as she goes! When they reach their destination, it's time to slip out the back door and go straight down the silly slide.

Marina Anchors Bubble Fun

Splish-splash in the bath with Marina Anchors Bubble Fun playset. Marina loves to play in the tub with her pet whale. She pretends she's in a real boat sailing to faraway lands. Along the way, she meets so many new sea animal friends! But when she spots a distant coast, she turns the boat right back around. Who wants to go ashore when you can sail the shining sea?

Camping with Sunny

Set up your tent and gather around the fire—it's time to go camping with Sunny Side Up! Sunny knows how to toast the tastiest marshmallows. And when her friends have had their fill, they sing silly songs and tell spooky stories until it's time to snuggle up in their sleeping bags.

Sew Sweet Playhouse

Welcome! It's home, sew sweet home at the Lalaloopsy Sew Sweet Playhouse! This adorable three-story house is the perfect place for all your mini Lalaloopsy dolls to play together! They can pitch in and plant beautiful flowers in the garden with Blossom Flowerpot. Or they can join Bea Spells-a-Lot on the porch swing as she talks about her favorite books! The pets love the playhouse, too! They take the pet elevator up to the attic and play hide-and-seek together!

Once, Blossom invited every friend in Lalaloopsy Land to come over for a big barbecue! Pepper Pots 'n' Pans flipped burgers, while Pix E. Flutters bounced around and served lemonade. Misty Mysterious put on a magic show, Tippy Tumblelina showed off a new dance, and Peanut Big Top juggled and told jokes. Together, they all played tag until it got dark. It was a fantastic good time!

Mail
A+

Vroom! Vroom! Roll through town in style with Charlotte Charades in her RC Cruiser! This sew cute convertible fits two, so she can ride in style with a friend. There's no end to the places they could explore!

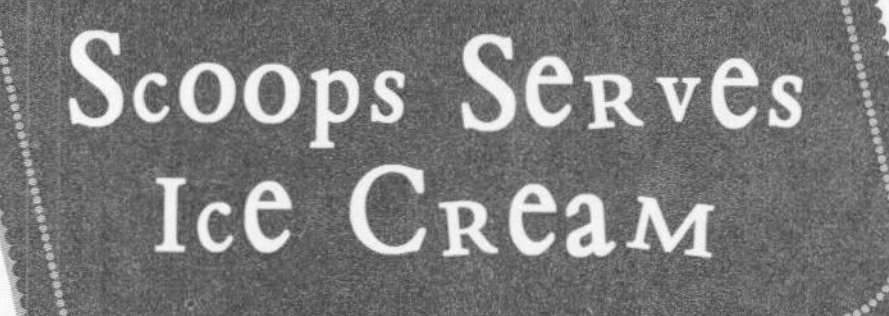

Scoops Serves Ice Cream

Scoops Waffle Cone loves serving ice cream to all her friends. She has sew many different flavors to choose from — yum!

It's a day of carnival fun for the Lalaloopsy! They're taking their pets to the Silly Funhouse for giggles galore. It's going to be sew fun!

Silly Funhouse RC Cruisers

It's double the driving fun! Cake Dunk 'N' Crumble and Spot Splatter Splash can't wait to explore Lalaloopsy Land in these two remote-controlled clown-car cruisers. So get ready to hit the road!

Tippy's Ballet Recital

Tippy Tumblelina is putting on a recital for all her friends! Help her practice her pliés so she's ready for her performance, and then take a seat behind the velvet ropes. It's going be sew spectacular!

Pet Parade

Chugga-chugga, choo-choo! The Lalaloopsy pets are on parade in their very own train. Each pet has its own car. All aboard!

The Lalaloopsy dolls are your key to everlasting friendship and fun! With your imagination and love, you can unlock their magical world filled with exciting new adventures. Once you've spent time getting to know them, you'll see why they are sew magical and sew cute!